My Family's Soybean Farm

To Adam, whose questions about farming inspired me to write this book.

~ K.O.

To my dad, Carroll, the hardest working farmer I know.

~ J.H.

FEEDING MINDS PRESS

American Farm Bureau Foundation for Agriculture®

ISBN 978-1-948898-08-9

Library of Congress Control Number: 2021949335

Book design by Mary A. Burns   Edited by Emma D. Dryden

Printed in the United States of America

First Edition

10 9 8 7 6 5 4 3 2 1

We plant the soybeans in the spring. Our tractor pulls a planter and the planter drops soybean seeds into the soil.

A few days later, the seeds sprout and soybean plants begin growing.

All plants need sunlight and water.

Leaves absorb sunlight.

Stem

Roots gather water and nutrients.

Soybean plants have many tiny white or purple flowers. The flowers are about the size of your pinky fingernail.

After the flowers wilt, pods begin to grow. The pods are the fruit of the soybean plant.

Each pod usually has three beans inside. The beans are the seeds. They are harvested and used for other purposes like food for humans or animals.

In the summer, we use remote-controlled drones to check our soybeans.

We check to make sure our soybean plants are healthy. Bugs, weeds, and fungi can damage our soybeans.

The drones fly over the fields and take pictures or videos of the soybean plants.

We also walk through our fields to check the soybean plants. This is called "crop scouting." Uh oh! These soybean plants have been damaged by aphids. We use a safe, gentle bug spray to get rid of harmful insects.

In the fall, the soybean plants finish growing. When the soybean pods are dry and hard, we harvest them.

There are several steps to remove the soybeans from the field. In the past, farmers had to do each part separately.

But our combine does all the steps. It cuts the stem. It takes the plant inside the machine. It cracks the pods and separates the beans from the rest of the soybean plant.

The beans are put in wagons and taken to grain bins. The grain bins keep the soybeans dry until we sell them.

We sell our soybeans to a processor.
The processor makes the beans
into food for animals.

Soybeans have a lot of protein in them. Protein helps animals grow.

Our pigs eat food that contains crushed soybeans.

Turkeys, chickens, cattle, and fish also eat food made with soybeans.

Charlie's pet food even has soybeans in it!

CHARLIE

Farmers in the United States grow
a lot of soybeans. Some of the
soybeans are used by American
farmers and processors.

Most soybeans are used for livestock food, but we eat food made from soybeans, too.

Have you ever tried soy sauce? It's made from soybeans and it's delicious! Oil from soybeans can be made into cooking oil or into biodiesel fuel.

Soybeans are also used to make ink, crayons, and glue.

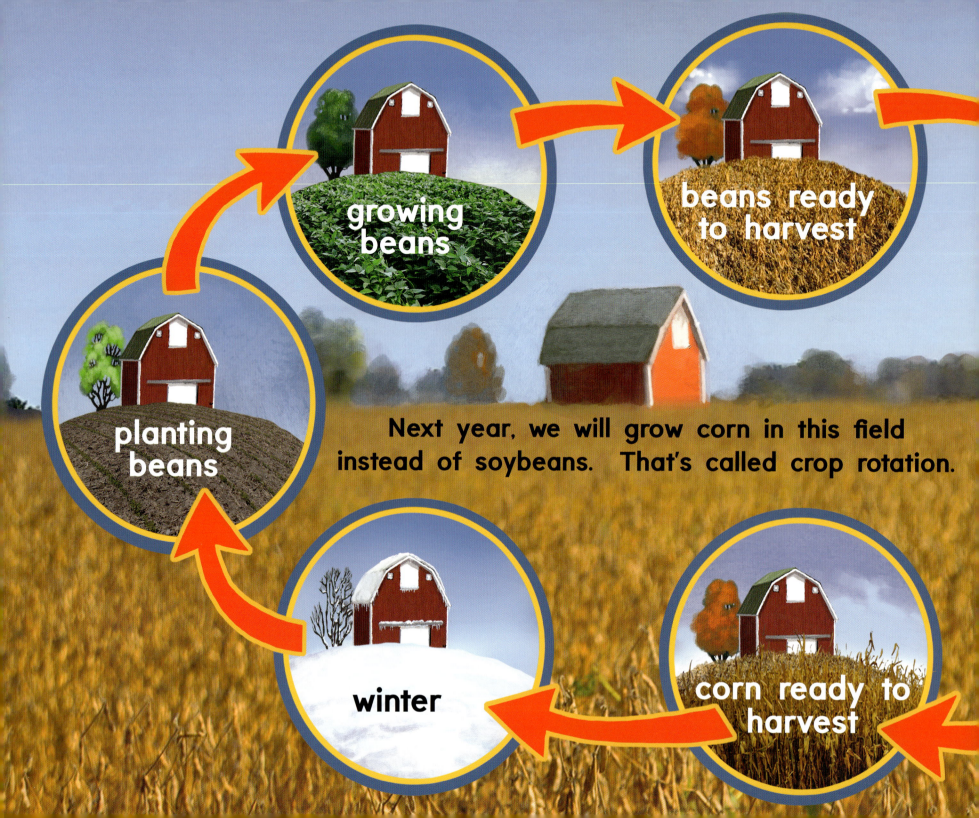

growing beans

beans ready to harvest

planting beans

Next year, we will grow corn in this field instead of soybeans. That's called crop rotation.

winter

corn ready to harvest

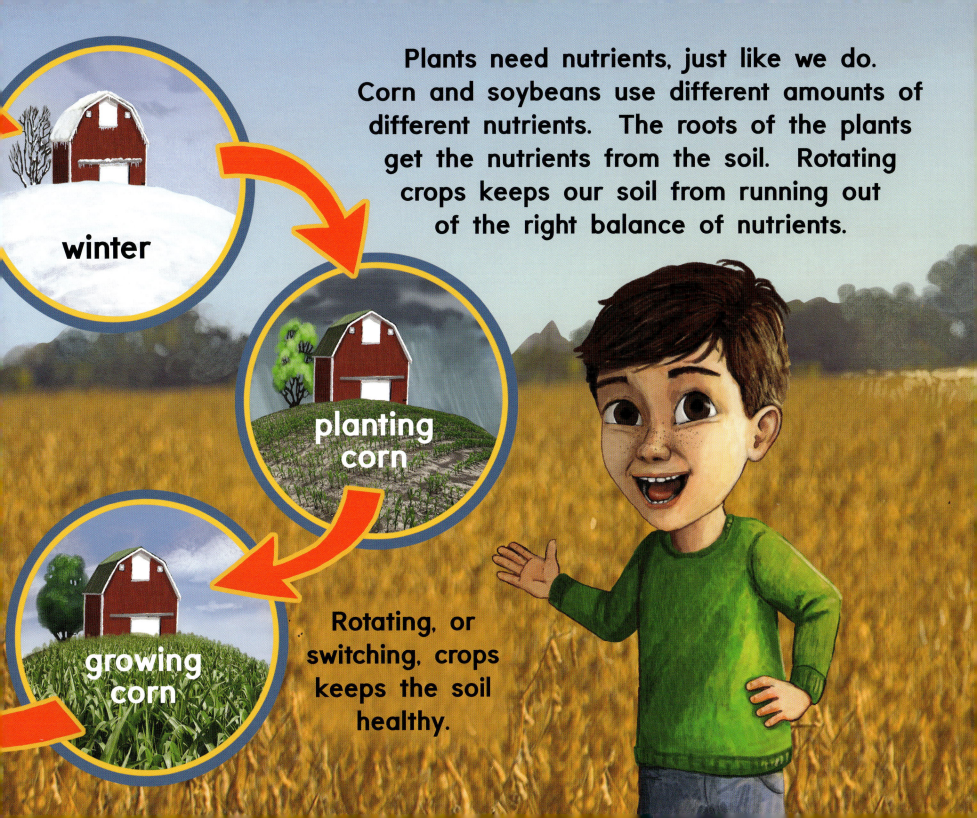

Plants need nutrients, just like we do. Corn and soybeans use different amounts of different nutrients. The roots of the plants get the nutrients from the soil. Rotating crops keeps our soil from running out of the right balance of nutrients.

winter

planting corn

growing corn

Rotating, or switching, crops keeps the soil healthy.

Mom and dad are farmers,

my grandparents were farmers,

and my great-grandparents were farmers.

GLOSSARY

Aphid: a tiny bug that can damage crops

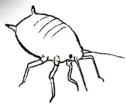

Biodiesel: fuel that can be made from soybeans and used in diesel engines

Combine: a machine that harvests crops

Crops: plants raised for food

Crop rotation: planting different crops each year

Drones: remote controlled, flying robots with cameras; also called UAVs, or unmanned aerial vehicles

Farmer: someone who grows food or raises livestock

Fuel: a material that produces heat or power, like gasoline

GLOSSARY

GPS: global positioning system; a network of satellites that communicate with receivers on the ground to determine exact locations on Earth

Harvest: gathering crops

Livestock: farm animals, including cattle, hogs, sheep, goats, poultry and others

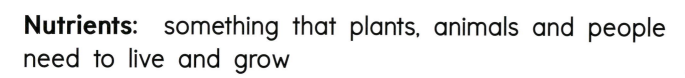

Nutrients: something that plants, animals and people need to live and grow

Growing up, KATIE OLTHOFF dreamed of following in the footsteps of authors like Laura Ingalls Wilder, Lucy Maud Montgomery and Louisa May Alcott, who wrote fiction based on everyday life. After marrying a farmer and learning more about agriculture, Katie began writing (mostly non-fiction) articles and books about farming, and she has written for many different agriculture organizations and publications. Katie and her husband have three children and live on a turkey farm in central Iowa with their cat, Snuggles, and beagle, Charlie.

JOE HOX was born with a spade in one hand and a pencil in the other. He was raised on an Iowa farm where he spent his days vanquishing thistles and sketching critters. Today as an artist, he's moved to town, but he's still inspired by rows of corn and fluffy clouds over cow pastures. Joe has illustrated more than a dozen books, including *Zoe's Hiding Place* and *Farmer Gary's Birthday Adventure*.

For free educational activities

visit: www.feedingmindspress.com

The goal of FEEDING MINDS PRESS is to create and publish accurate and engaging books about agriculture.

Photo credits:

Photos on pages 3, 4, 5, 6, 7, 13, 17, 23, 24 and 25 by **Joe Hox** with a special thank you to Calvin Rozenboom, Sully Transport, and Two Rivers Cooperative for allowing Joe to photograph on their property.

Photo of Kinze planter on page 4 provided by **Kinze Manufacturing**.

Photots on pages 8, 9, 10, 11, 15, 18, 19, 24, 25, 27, 28, 29 and 30 provided courtesy of **United Soybean Board**.

Photo of soybeans on pages 9, 15, 18, 28 and 29 by **ithinksky/Getty Images**.

Photos on page 19: turkey photo **DarcyMaulsby/Getty Images**, feeding fish photo: **hdagli/Getty Images**,

Historical photos on page 14 from top to bottom: Photo courtesy of **Deleware Public Archives**, **Library of Congress**, LC-DIG-fsa-8a23799, and **Library of Congress**, LC-DIG-fsa-8c30949